Memoirs of a HAMSTER

By Devin Scillian and Illustrated by Tim Bowers

Sleeping Bear Press™
315 E. Eisenhower Parkway, Suite 200
Ann Arbor, MI 48108
www.sleepingbearpress.com

Printed and bound in the United States.

10 9 8 7 6 5 4 3 2 1

Library of Congress Cataloging-in-Publication Data

Scillian, Devin.
Memoirs of a hamster / written by Devin Scillian ; illustrated by
Tim Bowers.
p. cm.
Summary: "A pet hamster is enticed by the family cat to venture outside
his well-equipped cage to the sunroom only to very quickly discover life
outside his cage is not the best for him."—Provided by publisher.
ISBN 978-1-58536-831-0
[1. Hamsters—Fiction. 2. Cats—Fiction.] I. Bowers, Tim, ill. II.
Title.
PZ7.S41269Mfh 2013
[E]—dc23
2012033693

Night One

My life is perfect.

I have a bowl full of seeds, a cozy pile of wood shavings, and room to run.

I'm never leaving here.

Question: Who's the luckiest hamster in the world?

Answer: **ME!**

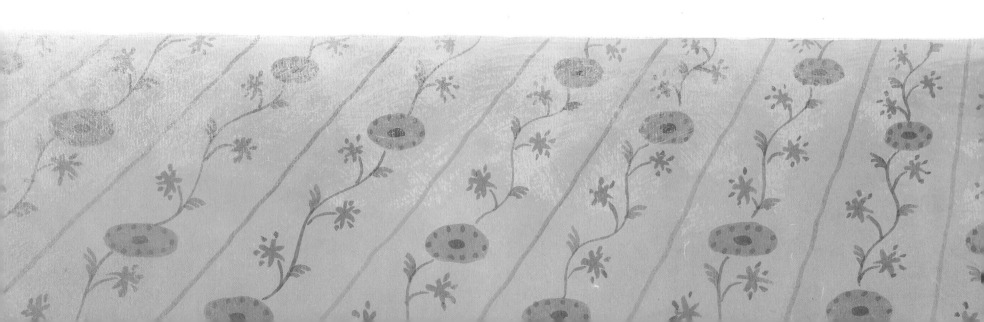

Night Two

I was just telling myself, "Seymour, you've got it made," when my exercise wheel was delivered. (I like to work out.) It's the best model around, the FuzzyBoy 360, shiny as a new dime and fast as lightning. I don't know how many miles I put in, but I was on that wheel all night!

Night Three

It took me a while to get the hang of my new water bottle, but it's great. It's important, too. A hamster has to stay hydrated.

Back to my wheel; I've got another hour to put in before daylight!

Night Four

Little Girl came by and gave me
a kiss on the nose. Nasty. Hello?
Ever hear of germs? But she also
gave me two yogurt drops.

Question: What's better than a yogurt drop?
Answer: TWO yogurt drops! I ate one and
tucked the other in my cheek to save for later.

This hamster has it going on.

Night Five

I was just climbing onto my wheel tonight when Pearl the Cat came by. "You know," she said, "you run for miles every night, but you never leave that cage. What's it all for?"

"I don't know," I said. "It's what hamsters do."

"What a complete waste of time," she said. "Have fun in your cage. I'm going to the sunroom."

Sunroom? What's a sunroom?

Night Six

Little Girl woke me up to clean my cage today. She kissed me on the nose again. Barf! She needs to knock that off. But while she was carrying me around, I realized there's a lot of house around me that I haven't seen. It seems to go on forever! I tried as hard as I could, but I couldn't see a sunroom.

Little Girl gave me a yogurt drop, and I completely forgot about the sunroom. Whatever a sunroom is, is it better than a yogurt drop?

Answer: **NO!**

Night Seven

I planned on running a marathon tonight, but my FuzzyBoy 360 is a little squeaky. Pearl came over to the cage looking a little annoyed. "You really need to get yourself out of there," she said.

"But why?" I asked. "I've got my wheel, I've got my seeds, I've got yogurt drops..."

"You wouldn't need a wheel out here," she said. "There's plenty of room to run. The staircase is made of sunflower seeds. And the sunroom is **filled** with yogurt drops."

As she was walking away she turned around and said, "Watch out for Hoover."

Hoover? Who's Hoover?

Night Eight

I didn't sleep a wink all day. Little Girl came by and kissed me on the nose—**YUCK!** And then I had a terrible workout. I just couldn't focus. How could I concentrate knowing what I know? Imagine…a whole staircase made of sunflower seeds! And the sunroom? Don't I deserve to be in the sunroom?

Buck the Dog came by to give my cage a sniff, and I said, "Buck, do you like the sunroom?"

Big, goofy Buck said, "I **love** the sunroom. It's so…sunny." And he trotted away.

Night Nine

No workout tonight.

I spent the whole evening putting together a plan.
I went over every square inch of my cage, and I think I've got it figured out.
Operation Tasty Treat is set for tomorrow night. Hello, staircase! Hello, sunroom!

Night Ten

Good ol' Seymour is one smart hamster!
My escape went like clockwork. I moved the seed dish. Then I was able to muscle the FuzzyBoy to the front of the cage. I had a little trouble climbing the outside of the wheel. It kept spinning and I wasn't getting anywhere. But sweet Pearl suggested I jam a sunflower seed at the side of the wheel, and it worked! After that, it was easy. I shimmied up the wheel and popped the lid right off.

Question: Who's going to eat every yogurt drop in the sunroom? Answer: **ME!**

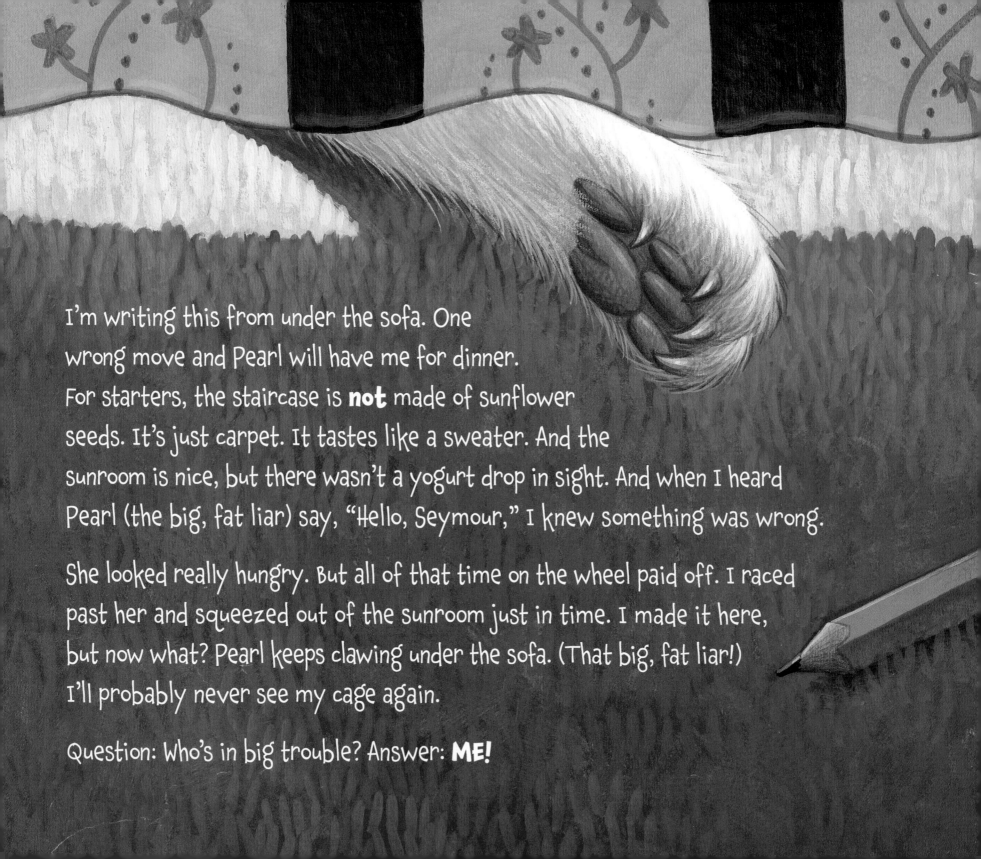

I'm writing this from under the sofa. One
wrong move and Pearl will have me for dinner.
For starters, the staircase is **not** made of sunflower
seeds. It's just carpet. It tastes like a sweater. And the
sunroom is nice, but there wasn't a yogurt drop in sight. And when I heard
Pearl (the big, fat liar) say, "Hello, Seymour," I knew something was wrong.

She looked really hungry. But all of that time on the wheel paid off. I raced
past her and squeezed out of the sunroom just in time. I made it here,
but now what? Pearl keeps clawing under the sofa. (That big, fat liar!)
I'll probably never see my cage again.

Question: Who's in big trouble? Answer: **ME!**

Night Twelve

I'm doomed. I'll never make it out of here alive.

I can see Pearl pacing back and forth. She says she's looking up recipes.

I tore a tag off the bottom of the sofa, found an old pencil, and wrote out my will. "I, Seymour Q. Hamster, being of tired mind and hungry body, leave my FuzzyBoy 360 to my 17 brothers. I leave my water bottle to my 22 sisters. And to my sweet mother and father, I leave the four yogurt drops hidden in the corner of my cage. I won't be needing them."

I sniffled a few times and fell asleep. "Goodbye, friends. I love you all."

Night Thirteen

So hungry and tired I could barely move, I heard Pearl purring the way she does when she sleeps. It was my only chance. I tiptoed out from the back of the sofa and headed straight for my cage. I was going to make it! But suddenly, there was a terrible noise. It sounded like a hurricane.

An enormous monster was coming right at me. I looked up at its terrible eyes and read the most frightening word: **HOOVER!** It was trying to suck me inside! Buck heard the commotion and started barking like crazy. That woke up Pearl, the big, fat liar, who hissed, "He's mine!" and started racing right toward me. Hoover had me by the tail, Pearl was swiping at me with her claws, and Buck was howling like mad.

I was a goner.

I closed my eyes and waited for it to be over.

And then came the sweetest thing I've ever heard.
"SEYMOUR!"
It was suddenly very quiet. Hoover, Pearl, and Buck stopped in their tracks. And one surprised but happy Little Girl got to me first. She kissed me on the nose, a lovely, beautiful, sweet kiss.

And I kissed her right back. Twice.

Night Fourteen

My life is perfect.

I have a bowl full of seeds, a cozy pile of wood shavings, and room to run.

I'm never leaving here.

Question: Who's the luckiest hamster in the world? Answer: **ME!**